# MAGIC GAME ADVENTURES

# POLAR EXPLORERS

by Jack D. Clifford

Illustrated by Russ Daff

W

FRANKLIN WATTS

LONDON • SYDNEY

Harry and Jade were playing a game.

They were trekking to the South Pole.

"I have an ice pick!" said Jade.

"I've got some ropes!" cried Harry.

Suddenly, a red light shone ...

Harry and Jade were

in the snow and ice.

"Where are we?" cried Harry.

"I think we're in the game!"

shouted Jade.

Just ahead of them stretched
a deep, wide ravine.

"Look!" cried Harry.

"There are some penguins!"

"Are they stuck?" asked Jade.

Soon some other explorers appeared. "Hello!" they shouted. "These penguins live in the colony on your side of the ravine. They must have got lost."

"Could we help them?" shouted Jade.

"We could try," shouted the explorers.

Harry had an idea. He threw
a rope across to the other side.

"Got it!" cried the explorers,

tying the rope to an ice pick.

"Throw a rope back with an ice pick and we'll tie it this side!" cried Harry.

14

"With a few ropes, we can make
a bridge for the penguins."

Soon, there were six ropes crossing the ravine. From each side of the ravine Harry, Jade and the explorers threw armfuls of snow onto the ropes until they had made a snow bridge.

One of the penguins carefully
tottered along the bridge.

Harry and Jade held their breath as the penguin got near to them.

"You made it!" cheered Jade as the

penguin slithered onto the ice beside her.

The other penguins soon followed and
crossed the bridge one after the other.

"Well done! Their chicks will be very pleased to see their parents," shouted the other explorers. "Can we leave this bridge here in case it happens again?"

But before Harry and Jade could reply,

a red light shone ...

... and they were back home.

"This is much warmer!" laughed Jade.

"Thank goodness!" cried Harry.

# PUZZLE TIME

Can you put these pictures

in the correct order?

TURN OVER FOR ANSWERS!

Tell the story in your own words

with YOU as the hero!

# ANSWERS

## The correct order is: c, a, d, b.

First published in 2011 by
Franklin Watts
338 Euston Road
London
NW1 3BH

Franklin Watts Australia
Level 17/207 Kent Street
Sydney
NSW 2000

Text © Jack D. Clifford 2011
Illustration © Russ Daff 2011

The rights of Jack D. Clifford to be
identified as the author and Russ Daff
as the illustrator of this Work have been
asserted in accordance with the Copyright,
Designs and Patents Act, 1988.

ISBN 978 1 4451 0309 9 (hbk)
ISBN 978 1 4451 0317 4 (pbk)

**Series Editor:** Jackie Hamley
**Series Advisor:** Catherine Glavina
**Series Designer:** Peter Scoulding

Printed in China

Franklin Watts is a division of Hachette Children's Books,
an Hachette UK company. www.hachette.co.uk